The Big Yellow House
on
Grandfather's Farm

COUSIN LILLIAN COMES TO THE FARM

Back Road to the Woods
Apple Orchard
Bees
THE BIG YELLOW HOUSE
Well House
Garage
Tool Shed
Garden
Country Road No. 614
THE BIG YELLOW HOUSE ON GRANDFATHER'S FARM
A Plat of the Main House and Its Surrounding Outbuildings as It Appeared in 1932

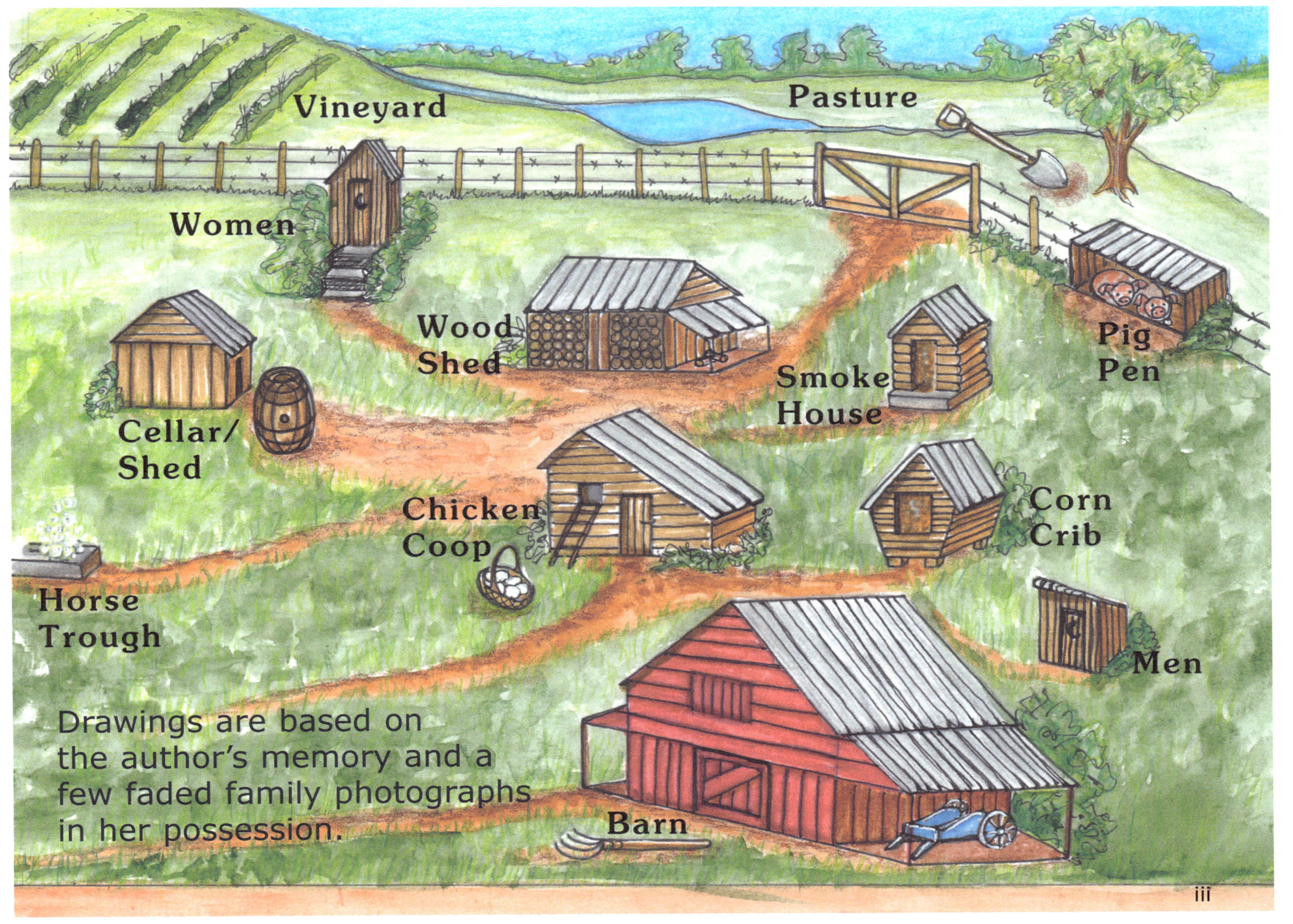

Vineyard
Pasture
Women
Wood
Shed
Pig
Pen
Cellar/
Shed
Smoke
House
Chicken
Coop
Corn
Crib
Horse
Trough
Men
Drawings are based on
the author's memory and a
few faded family photographs
in her possession.
Barn

Each day of that summer
While doing our chores,
We spun webs of memories
To last ever more.

— from "Chores"

The Big Yellow House
on
Grandfather's Farm
COUSIN LILLIAN COMES TO THE FARM

Agnes Evans Gish

HERITAGE BOOKS
2018

HERITAGE BOOKS

AN IMPRINT OF HERITAGE BOOKS, INC.

Books, CDs, and more—Worldwide

For our listing of thousands of titles see our website
at
www.HeritageBooks.com

Published 2018 by
HERITAGE BOOKS, INC.
Publishing Division
5810 Ruatan Street
Berwyn Heights, Md. 20740

Heritage Books by the author:

The Big Yellow House on Grandfather's Farm: The Journey

The Big Yellow House on Grandfather's Farm: Cousin Lillian Comes to the Farm

The Sweet Springs of Western Virginia: a Bittersweet Legacy

Virginia Taverns, Ordinaries and Coffee Houses:
18th–Early 19th Century Entertainment Along the Buckingham Road

Illustrations on pages ii, iii, iv, and 22 by Debbie Riley.

International Standard Book Numbers
Paperbound: 978-0-7884-5844-6

DEDICATION

To my Cousin Lillian who shared these childhood memories

ILLUSTRATIONS
Agnes Evans Gish
Debbie Riley
Kathryn Grace Odom

ACKNOWLEGEMENTS

Special thanks to those who
helped make this second
book possible:

Gregory F. Pastor
Julie Gish Norris
Loraine Wilson
Desiree Holmes Scherini
Carol Campbell
Kathy Byus

PROLOGUE

At the turn of the 20th Century, ships like the *S. S. Kaiser Wilhelm der Grosse* [Emperor William the Great] were bringing vast numbers of Eastern and Central European immigrants in to America. My grandfather, Vincent Frödl and my grandmother, Theresia Bednar, natives of the Kingdom of Bohemia (Czechoslovakia) were among them.

My grandparents married in Wisconsin and moved to Omaha, Nebraska, where grandfather found work in the meat packing industry. About this time, Col. Henry W. Weiss of Farmer's Land and Insurance Company in Emporia, Virginia, devised a plan for selling idle plantation land to these immigrants who had the skills to farm small tracts of land with only family labor.

Col. Weiss placed an advertisement in *The Virginian* and distributed it in the northern states where they had settled. The response was so great that he built a hotel to accommodate the immigrants traveling to Virginia in hopes to buy land. By 1903 over thirty-four parcels of land had been purchased by men with last names such as Byrna, Sapko, Veliky, Blaha and Frödl. Soon the White Anglo-Saxon Protestant town of Emporia was surrounded by immigrant families. By 1908, my grandfather, now a naturalized citizen, had paid off his note for the hundred acres of land he bought and moved his young family from Omaha to Virginia.

The farm was located on a secondary dirt road, Route 614, seven miles equidistant between the towns of Emporia and Jarratt. By the time I arrived in 1932, the road was still unpaved but the farm had reached its peak of development. The two-story house and accompanying well house that grandfather built had been painted yellow along with the garage that protected the Model-T Ford. The first-built log cabin had become the kitchen that adjoined the big house. Today nothing remains to show where the "Big Yellow House on Grandfather's Farm" once stood. Lightning struck, burning the house down leaving weeds, wild brush and a new growth of trees to reclaim the land.

x

In 1932, the United States has already undergone three years of havoc wrought by the economic crisis known as the "Great Depression" leaving many fractured families like mine in its wake. My mother and I were among those families living in New York. Mother was finding it difficult to find work suitable with a five-year old daughter in tow.

"Come home!" her parents pleaded again and again. Finally, in the late spring of 1932, she sent me on ahead while she tidied up her affairs.

When I met my grandparents for the first time, it did not matter whether I could understand them. Their big hugs mingled with the aroma of grandma's Kolache baking in the cast iron cook stove told me I was home. I spent my days helping grandma with little chores or following grandpa around the farm. Grandpa and grandma knew, however, that I needed someone my own age to play with. That person was my cousin Lillian. She brought her Baby Doll and I had my Raggedy Ann, but we soon tired of playing with dolls.

"What shall we do today?" and "What shall we play?" became our daily mantra. One day we'd be down in the root cellar or up in the hay loft. The next, we'd help grandma gather eggs from the hens or carry her letter addressed to her home town of Jamné in the "Old Country" to the mailbox that stood at the end of the dirt road.

Each night, after the animals had been fed, we had eaten our supper and washed the dishes, grandma would carry the kerosene lantern in to the dining room of the main house to listen to the radio for news about FDR's "New Deal." Lillian and I would scamper up the narrow steps to our room under the tin roof to sleep and spin webs of happy memories to store for reminiscing when we grew old.

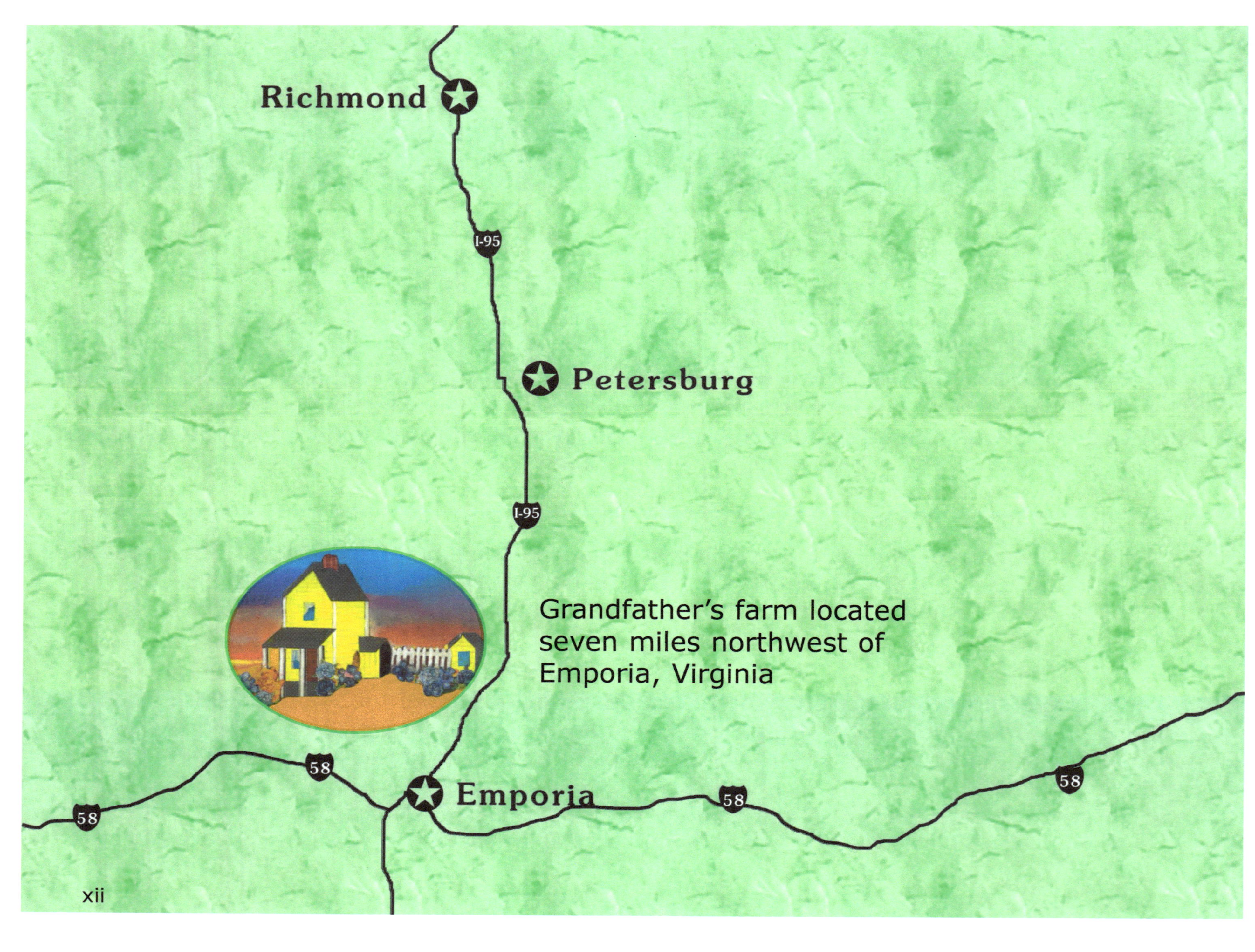

Richmond
I-95
Petersburg
I-95
Grandfather's farm located
seven miles northwest of
Emporia, Virginia
58
58
58
58
Emporia

GLOSSARY

GERMAN PHRASES

Meine Liebste Agnes [my-ne] [leeb-stuh] [Ag-nez] My dearest Agnes

Oh meine lieben Enkelkinder [oh, my-ne] [leeb-en] [en-kel-kin'-der]
Oh, my dear grandchild

Die Hausfrau [dee-house-frow] The Housewife (a German-language newspaper)

CZECH

Kolache   [ko-lá- chee]   sweet roll

Jamné   [yahm'-nay] Czech village

AMERICAN

VICTROLA - a phonograph machine from the Victor Talking
Machine Company, Camden, NJ, for the mechanical recording
and reproduction of sound.

STEREOPTICON - a hand held slide projector that
combines two images to create a three dimensional
effect, or makes one image dissolve into another.

PUMP ORGAN - a type of free-reed organ that generates sound as
air flows past a vibrating piece of thin metal, called a reed.

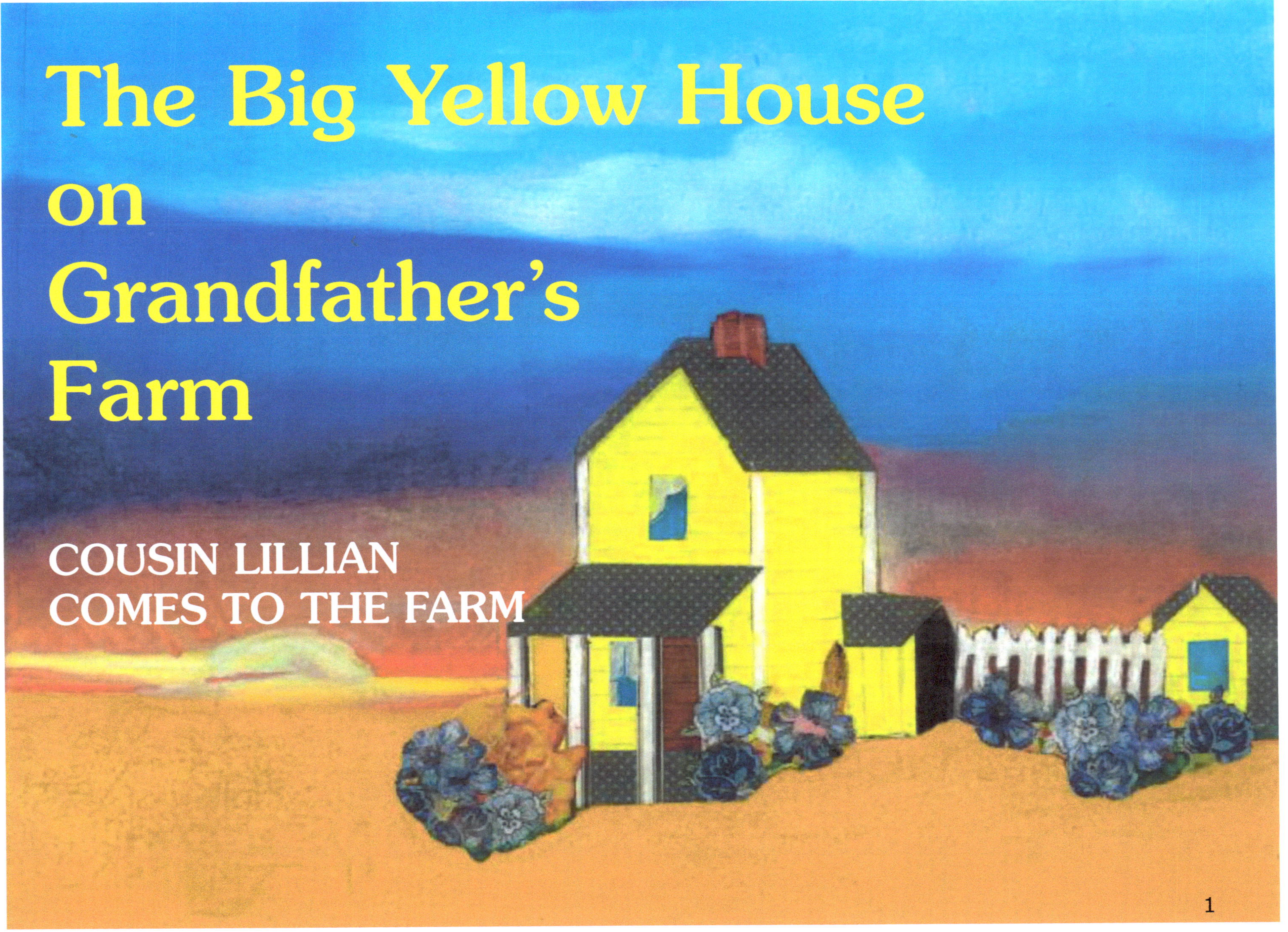

The Big Yellow House on Grandfather's Farm
COUSIN LILLIAN COMES TO THE FARM
1

COUSIN LILLIAN

"Meine Liebste Agnes. You're here all alone.
You need a playmate. I know just the one."

Soon thereafter, down the dirt road
With dust blowing 'hind it, came a black Ford.

It was her Uncle Charlie coming from town.
He opened the car door and Lillian stepped down.

"Hello Cousin Lillian," Agnes said with a smile.
"My grandpa has told me you'll be here awhile."

"Want to play something? The grown-ups are talking.
Let's go to the parlor. Shh, no one is looking."

"In there's an organ. Me play? Not alone.
Here, sit on this stool and pretend it's your throne."

4

"Pull out the stops, play on the keys.
I'll pump the pedals." They soon heard it wheeze.

It squeaked, then it squawked, then
It stopped with a groan.
"I think it's 'bout time we left it alone."

"Look, here's something you hold to see through.
Let's put in these cards. Wow! What a swell view!"

"Come over here. It's a thing that needs winding.
If you put on a tube you can hear people talking."

"Listen, I found one about a red hen.
Henny Penny's her name. Want to hear it again?"

What fun they had that day in the parlor
With organ, stereoptigan and the Victrola.

BLACKBERRY PICKING

"Come children, come. We're going berry picking."
"Wear these long sleeves. They keep thorns from pricking."

They wandered along the path in the wood
Where blackberries grew so sweet and so good.

They filled all the small pails then heaped up the big ones.
Tonight they'll make cobbler and send Lillian's mom some.

THE MELON PATCH

"What shall we do today?
Let's have some more fun."

I know, the melon patch.
Let's find us a big one.
Here's one that looks ripe,
Break open the heart.

For eating, its heart is
the very best part.
"I know where you've been!"
Said grandma in embrace.
"You've melon juice
everywhere,
Not only your face!"

THE ROOT CELLAR

"What shall we do today? Play in the cellar?
Its coolness and dankness in summer are stellar."

"Grandpa stores wine there in a big barrel.
I dare you to go down and siphon a little."

"I watched grandpa do it, I think I know how.
You draw as you breathe in. Here, I'll show you how."

The little girls siphoned, then siphoned some more.
The wine started spilling all over the floor.

"How do you stop it?" Lillian cried out in fright.
Just then, a dark shadow appeared in the light.

Grandfather heard their cries through the door.
He corked up the barrel and mopped up the floor.

The girls tried in vain to get up and stand,
But strangely their legs disobeyed their command.

Grandpa chuckled and chuckled. Twas funny to see
His two little grand-daughters drunk as could be.

He picked up the one girl, then picked up the other
To take to their Grandma. She'd help them recover.

THERE'S A HOLE IN THE PASTURE
Adapted from children's song
There's a Hole in the Bucket

"There's a hole in the pasture, dear children, dear children.
There's a hole in the pasture, dear children, a hole."

We know that, dear Grandpa, dear Grandpa, dear Grandpa.
We know that, dear Grandpa, 'cause we dug that hole.

But why did you dig it, dear children, dear children.
But why did you dig in the pasture, that hole?

So we could go swimming, dear Grandpa, dear Grandpa.
So we could go swimming in the pasture in that hole.

Put the dirt back, dear children, dear children, dear children.
Put the dirt back dear children. Put it back in the hole.

The cows need the water, dear children, dear children.
The cows need the water that flowed past that hole.

Yes, we better get started, dear Grandpa, dear Grandpa.
Yes, we better start shoveling that dirt in the hole.

Now the water flows through it, dear children, dear children.
Now it flows through the pasture as it did before.

SUDS IN THE HORSE TROUGH

"Who put the soap suds in the horse trough?"
"We did, dearest Grandpa, is that not enough?"

"We only want to take a bath
Out here where there's some sun."

"Ach du liebe, Enkelin,
I hate to ruin your fun."

"But horses cannot drink soap suds,
Would make them sick to dying."

"We're truly sorry, Grandpa,
But you can't blame us for trying."

WILDFLOWERS

"What shall we do today?"
"Let's go to the pond,
And try to find tadpoles
For you to take home."

"I'd rather find wildflowers.
Do you know where some are?"
"I think so. Come on,
It's not very far."

The hooty old owl
From the tree-top
"Who who--ed"
At the two little girls
Gone into the wood.

"I'll keep my eyes open,
I'll fly high and low
And lead you to places
where
Wildflowers grow."

15

PUTTING ON A PLAY

"What shall we do?
On this bright, sunny day?"
"There's folks here a-visiting.
Let's put on a play."

"Let's give it outdoors.
We can stand on the porch."
"Let's charge them a penny.
Don't think that's too much."

They found some old dresses,
High heels, and some hats,
They entered the porch 'round which
Visitors sat.

One acted like Garbo.
The other, Clara Bow.
Altogether, they were stars
Of the penny front yard show.

FUN IN THE HAY LOFT

"What shall we do today? What shall we play?"
"I know what I'd like to do. Jump in the hay."

"We'll climb up the ladder, then jump down the chute.
With hay in your hair, I bet you'll look cute."

"Don't be a scaredy-cat. Watch where you step."
And with that, the biggest girl down the chute leapt.

She'd not seen the pitch fork that stood in the way
Of Lillian, who made the next leap onto hay.

Lillian screamed out. Her foot had been pierced.
Twas no use to tug at it. Bleeding was fierce.

Agnes ran to get grandpa at work in his shed.
She told him what happened, how Lillian's foot bled.

To grandma he carried her. It wasn't a joke that
Lillian could sicken from rust on that fork.

"I told you two girls not to play in the loft,"
He said in his stern voice. "Once was enough."

"I'm sorry, I'm sorry," Little Agnes did cry.
Poor Lillian, it's all my fault if she should die."

He went for Doc Jarratt. With treatment most cunning,
In no time at all, she was 'bout the farm running.

CHORES

All was not play
On grandfather's farm.
From rooster's first crow,
Chores had to be done.

One daily chore
Was the walk down the road
For a penny post card,
Die Hausfrau, or Sear's catalogue.

They helped churn the butter
To put down the well
Where water kept cool
What they needed to sell.

They brought in the eggs,
They brought in some wood.
They washed all the dishes,
And dried them off good.

They washed the lamp chimneys
All blackened with soot.
Shined grandpa's church shoes
And cleaned off his boots.

Fed corn to the chickens,
Guinea hen, and geese.
The rest got some fodder
Once a day, sometimes twice.

Each day of that summer, while doing their chores,
They spun webs of memories, to last ever more.

SUMMER'S END

The crickets were bowing their leg violins,
Ceaselessly, endlessly in summer's warm wind.

The sound of the apple's loud plop from the tree,
Signaled the time they'd no longer be free.

Agnes was ready to start the first grade.
Lillian would have to go home with her dad.

One day thereafter, down the dirt road,
Dust blowing behind it, came the black Ford.

"Good-bye, dearest Lillian."   Agnes wiped on her sleeve
The tears that were falling to see her friend leave.

"Good-bye dearest Agnes. We did have great fun.
I hope I can come back next summer again."

Next summer did come, like night follows dawn at
THE BIG YELLOW HOUSE ON
GRANDFATHER'S FARM.

About the Author

In 1932, a night's trip by train, a big house painted yellow, and a German-speaking grandfather and a Czech-speaking grandmother, changed the course of life for author Dr. Agnes Evans Gish, then five. Her vivid memory of the occasion inspired her latest book, *The Big Yellow House on Grandfather's Farm*, written with the adult readers in mind, but meant to be shared with children. Dr. Gish is also an author of three historical books, *The Sweet Springs of Western Virginia* (Heritage Books, 2007), *Virginia Taverns, Ordinaries, and Coffee Houses* (Heritage Books, 2005), and *Hobson's Chapel* (Deitz Press, 1997). She also published numerous newspaper and magazine articles such as "A place of considerable trade for its size" *Virginia Cavalcade* (Vol. 50, Number 2, Spring 2001) and "A Victorian Parlor Piano" *Antiques & Collecting Magazine* (1996).

Dr. Gish holds degrees from the College of Notre Dame of Maryland, Virginia Commonwealth University, and obtained a Doctorate of Education from the University of Northern Colorado.

She now resides at Knollwood, a military retirement community located in Washington, D.C., where, at the age of ninety, she continues to write, paint and direct the Knollwood Singers' annual creative musical productions.